Welcome back, young apprentices and Jedi Masters! I'm so pleased to be seeing all of your friendly faces and cranial ridges and tentacles again, and I can feel the Force flowing through all of you as our campus is once more filled with the joys of discovery. But take care to remember that the path to becoming a Jedi is now and has always been full of challenges, and not all of them are joyous.

Having said that, please consult your student datapads for some new campus policy updates, particularly the section on the explicit prohibition against keeping wild animals in the dormitories. This also applies to very cute ones. Thank you and may the Force be with you!

Yarael Poof

Yarael Poof

AT LAST, JEDI

Jarrett J. Krosoczka & Amy Ignatow

Scholastic Inc.

For Zozo, Lucky, and Xavi
—Jarrett

To all the strong women who told me,
OF COURSE YOU NEED TO
WRITE A STAR WARS BOOK.
—Al

Published in the UK by Scholastic Children's Books, 2020
Euston House, 24 Eversholt Street, London NWI IDB
A division of Scholastic Limited

London ~ New York ~ Toronto ~ Sydney ~ Auckland
Mexico City ~ New Delhi ~ Hong Kong

SCHOLASTIC and associated logos are trademarks and/or
registered trademarks of Scholastic Inc.

First published in the US by Scholastic Inc., 2020

ISBN 978 0702 30075 2

A CIP catalogue record for this book is available from the British Library.

Printed by CPI Group (UK) Ltd, Croydon, CR0 4YY
Papers used by Scholastic Children's Books are made from wood
grown in sustainable forests.

2 4 6 8 10 9 7 5 3 1

www.starwars.com

www.scholastic.co.uk

HEPTADAY

It feels good to be back on Jedha, even though it took Q-13 all of two nanoseconds to start ordering me around.

Q-13, it's so good to see you!

I know. Now pack up, we're leaving in twenty minutes.

Q-13 totally missed me.

Even though it was nice to be home on Naboo, I'm really glad to be back on Jedha. When I'm on my home planet, I'm just plain old Christina Starspeeder whose mom makes her clean the algae off of the swamp runner. Here, I'm Christina Starspeeder, Jedi Apprentice.

And don't forget to scrub the sleeping berth on the Faravahar, before we leave. It still smells like juvenile nexu.

Oh, COME ON.

GALAXY FEED

6 Amazing Things to See and Do at Jedi Academy's Coruscant Campus

1. Meet with your favorite Jedi heroes!

2. Spend time in the tranquil herbarium!

3. Visit the fascinating Hall of Lightsabers!

4. Try to lift Master Yoda's favorite rock without using the Force!

5. Marvel at the majestic hallways of the nearby Jedi Temple (by appointment only)!

6. Taste-test exotic cuisines of the universe in the cafeteria!

GALACTIC ZOOLOGY TODAY

GUTKURR: FEROCIOUS PREDATOR OR USEFUL SECURITY PATROL?

By D'ian Afos

"A trained gutkurr is a friend in dark times."
—ancient Onderonian proverb

Native to the harsh terrain of Ryloth and Onderon, the insectoid carnivorous gutkurr is not the most obvious choice for a pet; they are enormous, highly dangerous, and they eat people. But if you are able to look beyond these obvious deficiencies you will find a creature of great strength and intelligence.

Gutkurrs are the second-most dangerous predator on Ryloth, second only to the vicious lyleks (although I don't quite know how this distinction was made—an encounter with either of these creatures in the wild will most likely result in being torn limb from limb and eaten). Like lyleks, gutkurrs have a hard exoskeleton that is resistant to blaster fire. Unlike lyleks, however, a gutkurr can be trained, provided the trainer is very, very brave and/or foolish. Once trained, a gutkurr will use its natural intelligence to defend its master.

But is it worth it? Notable fan of gutkurrs, Deemul the Hutt, believes so. "On one hand we have lost a few trainers, but having a stable of trained gutkurrs really keeps undesirables out of my compound where only totally legal things happen."

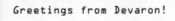

Greetings from Devaron!

We're in the middle of Devaron's rainy season, so it's pretty wet, and also soggy, and everything I own is extremely moist, but who cares, Master Iyawa just told me that we're heading to Coruscant for some big-deal meeting and you're going to be there, too! The Starspeeders, back together again on Coruscant! It's like we're coming home! Don't bring any weird animals.

Do you have any idea what this big Jedi meeting is about? Iyawa hasn't told me anything, but you know Jedi Masters, they're not exactly the chattiest. But she has told me . . . that she's going to let me pilot the *Tchagra*! See you soon!!!

Love,
Victor, your incredibly cool brother

P.S. Check out the hairstyle my friend J'eri gave me! I think I'm really beginning to fit in here.

Stargram

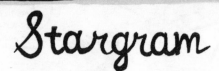

SpeedyC: Coruscant, here we come!
#Homecoming #JediAcademy

VICT-orious: Look who's piloting now!
Awwwwww yeah #Me #JustWantedToMakeThatClear

XelThaKiffar: Corsucant isn't kidding
around. #ecumenopolis

And this is my old school.

Hey, Elara!

Oh my goodness, Christina!

I'd heard you were coming back!

Where's Victor?

I don't see the *Tchagra* anywhere— if his Jedi Master is letting him pilot, he probably took it for a few loops around the sun.

That sounds about right.

You knew Christina while she was a student here?

Oooh, spill. Was she a massive dweebit? Like, Queen Empress of the Dweebits? Tell me EVERYTHING.

Sure did!

Uh, no, she was a hero and we all pretty much worshipped her.

Huh.

I find this extremely difficult to believe.

BEEP BOOP!

MONODAY

Showing my Jedha friends around Coruscant is so much fun!

BeepBoopBorksmit: Coruscant is AMAZING! Look at all the glorious technology!

FrkForce720: Very happy for the meditation spaces on campus. VERY.

Number1Lyndar: Okay, so this place is a little bigger than I expected . . . AND I LOVE IT.

DUODAY

Being back at my old Jedi Academy campus is so great! But also kind of strange. First, everything looks a lot smaller. I mean, not Coruscant itself, this city-planet is enormous, but the classrooms seem smaller and the students seem younger and the teachers seem a little less intimidating. Even Mr. Zefyr isn't that scary anymore.

He's still scary, sure, but he's definitely slightly less scary.

There were times last year where I would wish I was back here on Coruscant where everything was easier for me and I never felt like I had to constantly prove my worth. Everyone here knew me and had total confidence that I would one day be a great Jedi. That's an amazing feeling that I kind of miss—who wouldn't?

But now that I'm actually here, there's no way I'd want to go back to sitting in classrooms when I could be flying through the galaxy with Skia Ro.

THE DAILY MILLENNIUM

NOTORIOUS SITH LORD KRIO VIN ESCAPES FROM OOVO 4 DETENTION CENTER

In a daring early morning feat of physical prowess worthy of a gundark, the dangerous Sith Krio Vin, formerly known as Mervin Starspeeder of Naboo, escaped from the maximum security detention center on Oovo 4. Krio Vin had been previously sentenced to life imprisonment for theft, assault, child endangerment, and making heinous anti-Jedi threats.

This is a developing story . . .

QUADDAY

Oovo 4 is supposed to be one of the most secure prison facilities in the entire galaxy, so how could this have happened? How could my dad have gotten out? I thought we were safe from him. We were supposed to be safe!

It's not like I'd forgotten about Krio Vin. How could I when he sends a holomessage every few months? There was no way I was going to watch them, but now I wish I had. Maybe the holo talked about his plan for escape. I should have watched them!

Is this why all the Jedi Masters have been called to Coruscant? Did they know about Krio Vin before the *Daily Millennium*? Is this why all the teachers and masters have been so nice to me? Did they already know that my terrible father had escaped?

I need to find Victor. He's got to hear this from me first.

Before I could find my brother we were all called into the auditorium to meet. I kept looking around the room but I guess Victor hadn't arrived yet.

Principal Mar addressed the gathered Jedi and, as always, I took copious notes.

Welcome, Jedi Masters and apprentices, it is wonderful to see you all and I wish it could be under better circumstances. As most of you know by now, the Sith Krio Vin has escaped from his confinement on Oovo 4. He is very powerful and dangerous and wanted all over the galaxy for his crimes, and so we thought it best to bring all of the students and apprentices together to the secure Coruscant campus under the protection of Yoda while the other Masters work together to find the Sith.

We realize that some of you may have personal feelings on this matter and want to help, but Krio Vin has become very strong and the Masters need to be able to focus on dealing with him without worrying about you.

The good news is that we have a new grav-ball court which you may all feel free to partake in. We'll let you know when we find Krio Vin.

GALAXY FEED

Kashyyyk Journal: Cutting Edge Wookiee Architect Considers Building a Home at the Base of A Tree

Grav-Ball Semi-Finals: Is This Finally the Year for the Bespin Beldons?

Add Zest to Your Gornt Meat (and your life!)

GALACTIC ZOOLOGY TODAY

GALACTIC ZOOLOGY TODAY

GUNDARKS, THE FEROCIOUS PRIMATES OF
VANQOR
By D'ian Afos

Vanqor is not a tourist destination.
Its terrain is rocky and more often
than not beset by massive silica-dust
storms, making it unfriendly and nearly
uninhabitable. And from this unwelcoming
place comes a most unwelcoming creature:
the agile, extremely strong, four-armed,
sixteen-clawed gundark.

Those who have been intrepid enough to
find themselves on Vanqor have naturally
gravitated toward the planets complex
system of caves in order to escape the
dust storms. Unfortunately, these same
caves are also the perfect place to
accidentally fall into a gundark nest.
And rest assured, this is the last place
anyone would want to be, unless they
like to be cuddled . . . TO DEATH.

PENTADAY

After I told everyone who my father was I felt a little bit better. I mean, of course they weren't going to suddenly hate me, I never thought they would, but I was worried they were going to pity me, which in a way would be worse.

But of course my friends were totally there for me, just like they've been there for me over the past two semesters. I should have had more faith in them.

I fought Krio Vin when I was still a student on Coruscant, and afterward I acted like sending my own father to prison didn't bother me. I had to act like that because Victor needed me to be his strong, big sister, but he's older now and I think I can be more honest with him. Battling Krio Vin was the hardest thing I ever had to do.

I wish Victor would show up already. We need to be together.

Stargram

JediAcademyCoruscant: This is Victor Starspeeder. If you have seen him, please immediately inform the nearest Jedi. #FindVictor

MAYATHEATER: My friend is missing and I have a bad feeling about it. #FindVictor

AxiNueFanatic: Oh Em GEE Victor's dad is a SITH he's not "missing" he's JOINED HIM wake up people. #FindVictor #SithFamilyStarspeeder

ArtemisCC: Victor Starspeeder is strong and kind and mostly smart and he will always choose to do what's right. #FindVictor

XelThaKiffar: @AxiNueFanatic Oh Em GEE go shove your head in a trash compactor. #NotHelping #FindVictor

LIL77: Be on the lookout for Victor Starspeeder. He is the brother of a friend and he is missing. #Find Victor

Come in, please, Christina.

We wanted to talk with you about what we know.

Alone.

They refused to stay outside.

I am but a machine here to serve at the will of my master.

Since when?

Mind this not. Talk with you about Victor, we will.

Do you have any idea where he could be?

We've managed to fix the damaged droid from the *Tchagra*, and they have informed us that the ship was attacked and boarded somewhere in the Corellian system.

Is someone going there to look for them?

Yes, but you needn't concern yourself with that. We just wanted you to know that we're following up on every lead to find your brother and Master Iyawa. But it's also come to our attention that your father has been communicating with you.

He's been sending me holomessages. But I never opened them.

Curious, you were not?

No! I didn't want anything to do with him!

We didn't say you did, but we had to ask.

Do you think I have any idea what he's up to? Because I don't!

Be still, young Jedi. Believe you, we do.

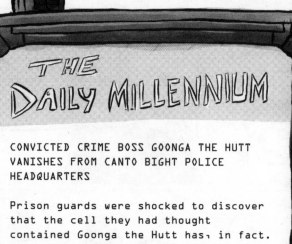

THE DAILY MILLENNIUM

CONVICTED CRIME BOSS GOONGA THE HUTT VANISHES FROM CANTO BIGHT POLICE HEADQUARTERS

Prison guards were shocked to discover that the cell they had thought contained Goonga the Hutt has, in fact. been home to a large pile of mashed stickli root fashioned to look like the feared gangster. Authorities have estimated that even with Goonga the Hutt's impressive appetite it must have taken up to five months to collect enough meals to make the life-sized sculpture.

"I just thought he enjoyed my cooking," sobbed Nursen Dogan, the prison complex's cook. "I made those meals with love. This hurts me in my feelings place."

It isn't currently known how long the mashed stickli root has been substituting for the Hutt, as the guards have admitted that he doesn't move much and normally smells even worse than an enormous pile of festering starch.

HEXADAY

How. Do. You. Lose. A. HUTT?!? Seriously??? I get that Krio Vin could escape from Oovo 4, he's a Sith Lord trained in the ways of the Force and also he's pretty athletic, but Goonga the Hutt weighed at least 1,400 kilograms and takes about an hour to move one hectometer.

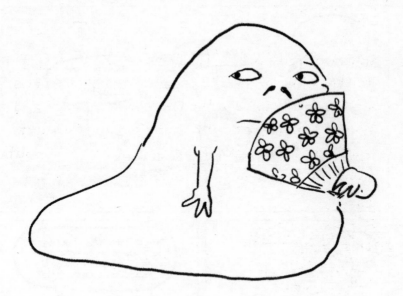

Somebody had to be helping him; there's no way he could get out by himself. But who would want to free Goonga the Hutt? And what is he going to do now that he's free? I know this for certain—he blames the Jedi (specifically me and my friends) for his imprisonment. I mean, sure, we defeated him but it's not like we forced him to do a bunch of crimes. Why can't criminals ever accept the consequences of their terrible actions?

Ugh. I don't think I'll ever be able to eat mashed stickli root again.

* We were traveling through the Quelli Sector when we were ambushed near Dathomir. A noxious gas was pumped into the *Tchagra* and Iyawa and young Victor fell into a stupor. The ship was boarded by Sith warriors who took my good masters and reprogrammed me to mislead you before setting the coordinates for the *Tchagra*'s autopilot for Coruscant. I beg you to forgive me for the deception.

49

I know that Victor is on Dathomir—I can feel it, and I'm sure that if we can get there in time my friends and I can save him, just like we stopped Goonga the Hutt on Canto Bight and I'gork Faul on Utapau. We're good at this sort of thing! But in order to get to Dathomir we need:

1. A ship
2. Someone to fly the ship

Kyt came up with the idea that we could just ... borrow the *Tchagra* for a bit. Sure, it looks like it's kind of falling apart but she believes that all of the damage is purely cosmetic and that Master Iyawa's ship is totally safe for intergalactic travel.

Which leads us to the teensy-weensy issue of who should be our pilot. Kyt would be the obvious choice, seeing how she understands machines and can fix anything, but we need her on hand to fix ... anything, so Xel has offered to be our pilot. It makes sense' seeing how he's flown a ship before. So we should be fine?

Hey, look, there's the Iktoetch toast I had for breakfast.
You don't chew your food enough.

MANHUNT CONTINUES FOR KRIO VIN

After a week of pursuit an elite team of Jedi Masters is still unable to find or apprehend the highly dangerous escaped prisoner Krio Vin. The hotline set up to give anonymous tips on his whereabouts has proven to be less than helpful, as panicked citizens are calling in with sightings of anyone with a beard. This has been particularly prevalent on Thisspias, where nearly everyone has a beard.

"We have been to Thisspias four times," a weary Jedi Master Mun told reporters, "and we're pretty sure he's not there. If you see someone with a beard, check to make sure they have legs. If they have a snake body instead of legs, it's probably not Krio Vin."

The search continues as Jedi Masters spread across the galaxy looking for the evil Sith Lord.

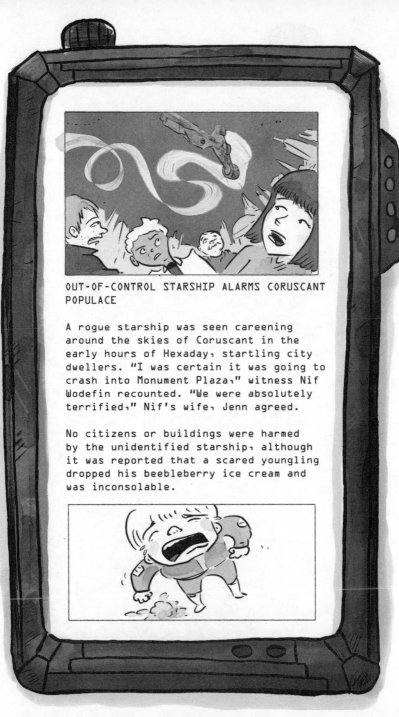

OUT-OF-CONTROL STARSHIP ALARMS CORUSCANT POPULACE

A rogue starship was seen careening around the skies of Coruscant in the early hours of Hexaday, startling city dwellers. "I was certain it was going to crash into Monument Plaza," witness Nif Wodefin recounted. "We were absolutely terrified," Nif's wife, Jenn agreed.

No citizens or buildings were harmed by the unidentified starship, although it was reported that a scared youngling dropped his beebleberry ice cream and was inconsolable.

GALAXY FEED

Should Children Be Allowed to Fly Starships? No, Say Nervous Parents and Everyone Else

Easy New Beard Styles for Every Occasion

One Service Droid's Quest to Find Love

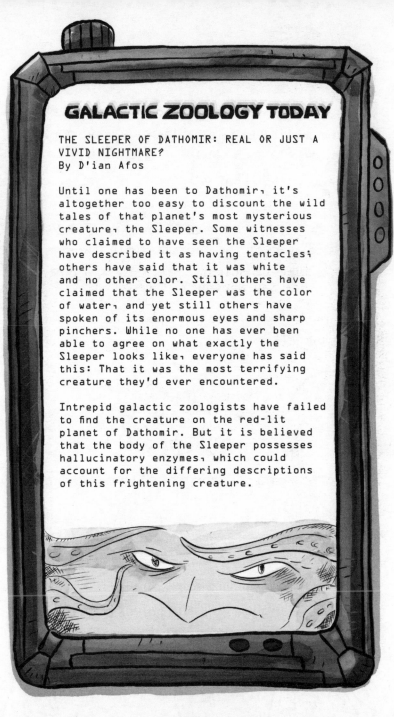

GALACTIC ZOOLOGY TODAY

THE SLEEPER OF DATHOMIR: REAL OR JUST A
VIVID NIGHTMARE?
By D'ian Afos

Until one has been to Dathomir, it's
altogether too easy to discount the wild
tales of that planet's most mysterious
creature, the Sleeper. Some witnesses
who claimed to have seen the Sleeper
have described it as having tentacles;
others have said that it was white
and no other color. Still others have
claimed that the Sleeper was the color
of water, and yet still others have
spoken of its enormous eyes and sharp
pinchers. While no one has ever been
able to agree on what exactly the
Sleeper looks like, everyone has said
this: That it was the most terrifying
creature they'd ever encountered.

Intrepid galactic zoologists have failed
to find the creature on the red-lit
planet of Dathomir. But it is believed
that the body of the Sleeper possesses
hallucinatory enzymes, which could
account for the differing descriptions
of this frightening creature.

PENTADAY

We've been in the *Tchagra* for what seems like forever and it's been a real learning experience.

Things We Have Learned

1. Flying a spaceship is pretty easy once you've taken off and set the coordinates! Although we're not 100% sure we're heading in the right direction.

2. We probably should have packed some supplies before we left.

3. There's not a whole lot to do when you're on a trip this long.

4. No one on this ship knows how to land a ship.

I wish we'd had more time to prepare. It's weird, because we were in such a hurry but now I've had a whole week of watching the stars go by to think about how messed up it is that my dad is out of prison and Victor has been captured. I'm so worried. What if Victor ends up siding with Krio Vin? They always had this bond, which is probably why he chose to kidnap Victor instead of me. I mean, I can't be upset that I wasn't the one kidnapped, right? That would be weird.

HEXADAY

So it turned out that Yoda saw us leaving on the *Tchagra* and had this amazing Jedi pilot follow us just in case we got into trouble (which we did). He's taking us back to Coruscant now, and it's pretty embarrassing to know that if he hadn't shown up we'd all be rancor breakfast on Dathomir. I never want to go back to that place.

But we saw my brother. WE SAW VICTOR AND IYAWA. I just knew they were on Dathomir. In fact, I've never been more certain of something in my life. Skia Ro was right when she told me that the Force connects every living thing.

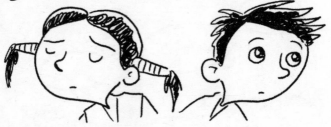

I'm upset that we weren't able to save Victor and Iyawa. But they're alive—at least we know that now. And I have no doubts that I'll be able to find them again. And I will.

But the fact remains that we did find Victor and Master Iyawa. My brother is still alive, and Goonga the Hutt has him. But why? And where is he taking them?

Returning to Coruscant empty-handed doesn't feel that great.

Everyone on the Coruscant campus is on edge—well, everyone who is still here. Parents have been pulling their kids out because they're afraid what happened to Victor will happen to them. It's too quiet.

I wonder what my mom would have done if this had happened to someone else while we were students here. Would she have pulled us out like all these other parents? She's always trusted that we would figure things out for ourselves (even when we were being sort of silly, like that time when we were kids and tried using the Force to make ourselves a snack). She always trusted us to make the right choices. Eventually.

angry, but impressed

Stargram

Jen-ra: I can't believe they're shutting down the Coruscant Campus! So sad. #FindVictor

JediAcademyCoruscant: The Jedi Academy at Coruscant remains open, although Padawans are free to take time to go home and be with their families if that's what they feel is necessary.

GravBallMom617: Enough is enough. If Krio Vin is grabbing kids, mine isn't going to be one of them! #CoruscantShutdown

It has been another week since we got back, and now, along with Yoda and Mr. Zefyr, we're practically the only ones left on the Coruscant campus. And even though we're on semester three of our apprenticeships Mr. Zefyr is insisting that we stay safe by remaining in our bunks at all times. This has led to some . . . irritability.

SHHOOP

IT'S KRIO VIN! LIGHTSABERS OUT!

Teeny, no, I'm not here to fight you.

Young Starspeeder, apprentices, down your weapons you must put.

Help, Christina and Victor's father will.

Weird.

Sooooo my escaped convict Sith dad is on campus, COOL, this all seems normal (yeah, right). Yoda says he's here to help us find Victor, but I can't help but think about that time when he chose the dark side over his family and remember how he tried to bring us over to the dark side and how I had to go undercover and pretend to be a Sith to take him down and I don't know, maybe the years of abandonment and him doing a bunch of evil and landing himself in prison and sending me creepy messages is not making me feel great about working with him?

Relatives are relative, when you think about it...

literally my least favorite person in the galaxy

perpetrator of awfulness

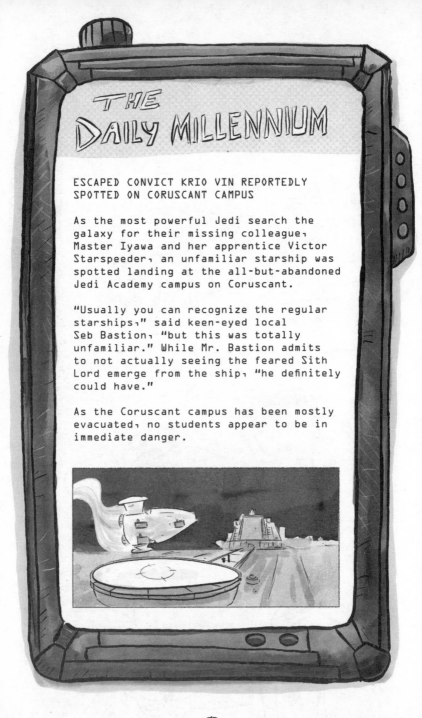

ESCAPED CONVICT KRIO VIN REPORTEDLY SPOTTED ON CORUSCANT CAMPUS

As the most powerful Jedi search the galaxy for their missing colleague, Master Iyawa and her apprentice Victor Starspeeder, an unfamiliar starship was spotted landing at the all-but-abandoned Jedi Academy campus on Coruscant.

"Usually you can recognize the regular starships," said keen-eyed local Seb Bastion, "but this was totally unfamiliar." While Mr. Bastion admits to not actually seeing the feared Sith Lord emerge from the ship, "he definitely could have."

As the Coruscant campus has been mostly evacuated, no students appear to be in immediate danger.

GALAXY FEED

Thinking of Becoming a Jedi? Consider Moisture Farming Instead!

Deemul the Hutt's 10 Tips for Surviving a Gutkurr Attack

How to Keep Your Blast Doors Looking Fresh After a Skirmish

Thank you for coming here. Krio Vin will now be speaking.

Thank you, Master Yoda. I know that most of you here don't know me, and if you do you don't trust me. That's fair.

But I have been hearing rumors of trouble brewing for some time, and I believe that my efforts to warn others have resulted in my son being taken away. Someone is trying to keep me quiet.

So Victor being kidnapped is your fault?

85

Wow.

Don't wow him, he's a Sith.

What? I can't respect the man's skills?

NO.

MONODAY

Guess who's got two thumbs and is stuck in a starship with her more-likely-than-not evil dad to save the brother that he's always wanted to turn to the dark side?

THIS GIRL!

I'm so glad that at least Xel is here so I'm not alone with Krio Vin.

So where are we headed?

So ... how's the apprenticeship with Skia Ro going?

Fine.

When I heard you were with her I was really impressed. She's formidable.

Well, when you risk your life by going undercover to take down your own estranged evil father, people tend to think you can handle a formidable Jedi Master.

I suppose so.

You're very strong.

Whatever.

Did Skia Ro teach you how to fight a gutkurr?

What? No. Why?

Well, gutkurrs are native to Ryloth and she's a Twi'lek so I assumed she was from Ryloth so . . . she'd know how to fight a gutkurr.

Master Ro has focused on teaching me to recognize the Force flowing through me and to be at one with all things so that I'm not seduced by the dark side.

Oh. Great.

THE DAILY MILLENNIUM

With infamous Sith Lord Krio Vin still on the loose it has been rumored that he has returned to Coruscant and the Jedi Academy campus where he met his downfall. But when asked, Principal Mar simply responded, "This is not the story you're looking for."

Other Jedi Masters still spread out over the galaxy in search of captured Jedi Iyawa, and her apprentice could not be reached for comment. Master Yoda, often considered to be the most eccentric of the Jedi Masters, would also not comment, unless answering every question with another question and then offering everyone homemade stew could be considered a comment.

Stargram

Coletastic: First Victor is gone, and now Christina? What's going on? #FindVictor #FindChristina

JediAcademyCoruscant: Contrary to rumors there have been no new notable incidents at the Coruscant campus.

BeepBoopBorksmit: Some times you have to improvise. #DroidRepair #CoruscantShutdown

XelThaKiffar: Christina Starspeeder can take care of herself. Don't mess with the apprentice who can tame a nexu. #ChristinaStarspeeder

FrkForce720: If we are at one with the Force, we have nothing to fear.

Number1Lyndar: Who here hates the Sith? #SithSmellLikeNerfs #Nerfstank

We managed to crash-land on a desert planet without damaging the ship too much, although we were half buried in sand until Krio Vin used the Force to lift us out.

He's really powerful. Scary powerful. He moved the entire ship like it was nothing.

And now it looks like we need to find some parts (Which makes sense, because our wing is pretty much off of the ship). Xel doesn't think it looks too bad, but he might just be saying that because he's a little embarrassed about FLYING US INTO A METEOR SHOWER.

Krio Vin says there's a settlement nearby, so he's going there and I'm going along because I don't trust him. Of course he's irritatingly thrilled that I'm coming along.

Wonderful! Do you want me to carry your pack? I can carry your pack.

I'm fine.

DUODAY

We've been walking through the desert for three hours and Krio Vin has been talking almost the entire time. I'm trying not to listen but he really, really wants to explain himself to me.

What am I supposed to say to that? That I understand and I forgive him? How can I?

Stargram

Gumbinno24: #KrioVin sighting on Ithor! Where's my reward money?

Hermelin39: Is it me or does this look like #KrioVin?

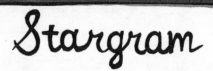

Kri-Ja: If #KrioVin is missing, and so is his son, and no one has seen his daughter, doesn't it stand to reason that they're all together? #SithLife

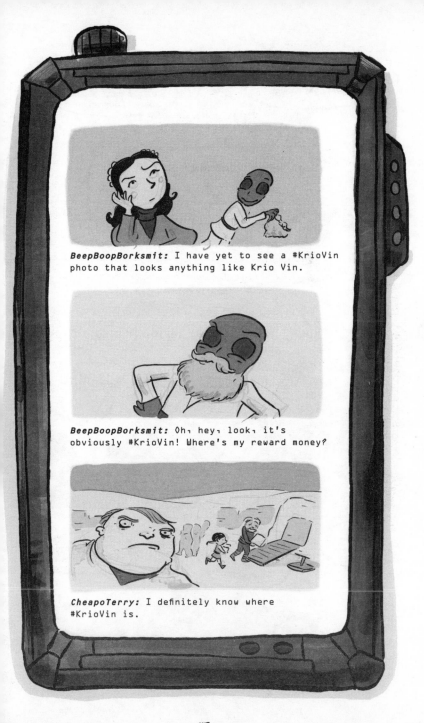

THE DAILY MILLENNIUM

KRIO VIN CAPTURED ON JAKKU!

After a harrowing battle witnessed by everyone at Cheap-O Terry's Scrap-O-Rama, dangerous escaped criminal Krio Vin was captured by bounty hunters on the desert planet of Jakku.

"He definitely put up a fight," said Terry Cheah, known locally as Cheap-O Terry. "Look at my salvage yard! There's hardly anything salvageable. Thank goodness I'll be getting the reward money for finding him, which I am hoping to get sooner than later."

With Krio Vin at the time of his capture was decorated Jedi apprentice Christina Starspeeder, although it is unclear as to whether she had been captured by the Sith, was in the process of capturing the Sith, or was working with the Sith. Cheap-O Terry himself was confused.

"She didn't seem to like him very much," Terry reported, but couldn't elaborate beyond, "she had kind of a sour face the whole time and maybe would have been prettier if she smiled."

Krio Vin is expected to be returned to his prison cell on Oovo 4, which by all accounts is a very unpleasant place to be.

CORUSCANT CAMPUS FOR SALE?

With the majority of the student population gone, local Galactic City property agents have begun to wonder if the Jedi Academy campus on Coruscant will soon be putting it on the market. The renowned campus has been at its current location for hundreds of years and Principal Mar was quick to dispel rumors of a sale.

"The campus will remain on Coruscant and although our students are currently on an unexpected vacation, we are certain they will return soon," the principal said, but popular real estate agent Trisdorfan Vannote was of a different opinion.

"It's a great location, and available properties on Coruscant are rare. If the students don't come back, there's absolutely no reason to hold on to all of this valuable land."

Neighbors expressed concern over the possibility of a sale, although some admitted it would be nice to have more parking spaces.

123

Master Ro!

Xel is still stranded in the desert!

Don't worry, Master Ojiee is already helping him with repairs. They will rendezvous with us in orbit of Batuu.

I had no idea what Master Ro was going to tell me, but after everything that's happened I was not expecting this. She actually told me ... that she was proud of me.

WHAT?

Master Ro told me that she was proud of me for being able to put aside my personal feelings in order to work well with Krio Vin. She was proud of me for remaining focused on finding Victor and Iyawa, and she acknowledged that it must have been really hard to spend all that time with Krio Vin without wanting to take some sort of revenge on him for what he'd done to our family.

It was really nice to hear, but I had to be honest with her.

Master Ro?

Yes, Christina?

I feel very conflicted about Krio Vin. I know he's done terrible things but I can feel the good in him. And I hate feeling it because it was easier to think of him as a lost cause.

This sounds very normal, Christina. You should feel conflict—very few people are ever purely evil, or purely good. The hard part is not letting the conflict overtake you, and you didn't. You remained focused, and that's why I'm proud of you.

GALAXY FEED

The Dark Side: What Is It Good For (Absolutely Nothing)

So You Suspect Your Neighbor Is a Sith

Fifty Ways to Love Your Loth-Wolf

GALACTIC ZOOLOGY TODAY

BEHOLD THE GENTLE NERF (BUT DON'T INHALE)
By D'ian Afos

If you are an omnivore or a carnivore, chances are that you've eaten some nerf meat. Who hasn't had nerf steak, or nerf nuggets, or a nice nerf stew? Everyone enjoys eating nerf, but not enough people like to think about where their food comes from, or the self-sacrificing herders who make it possible for the rest of us to enjoy a good meal.

Nerf herding is not for the faint of heart—or weak of stomach. Unlike most unpleasant smells, it is nearly impossible to become accustomed to the stench of a herd of nerfs. Just the stink of one juvenile nerf is enough to make most people experience a wave of nausea. And if the smell wasn't bad enough, a frightened nerf will shoot revolting gobs of mucus out of their nose and mouth! So a good nerf herder must not only be willing to put up with the hideous smell of the beast, but also be a calm and reassuring presence.

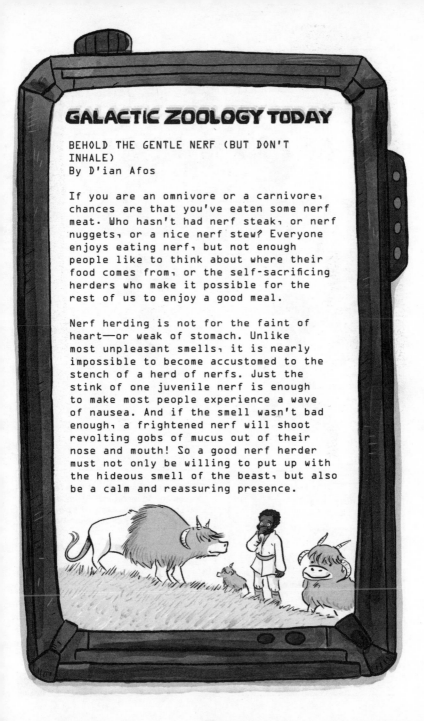

Where are we?

We are on the second moon of Batuu. Welcome to Jedi Base 18.

I've never heard of this place before.

That's a good thing. We set it up less than a year ago to monitor a disturbance in the Force. We suspect that a powerful Sith has taken residence on Batuu.

You can stop giving me the eyeball, Zefyr.

You may have Yoda fooled, but I know who you really are.

I'm not that person anymore, Zefyr.

So you admit that all those years ago, I was right?

You haven't changed a bit.

What are you talking about?

What were you right about?

He knows.

Get over it, Zefyr. My son is down there and we need to help him.

You can count on me. But for Victor and Iyawa's sake. Not yours.

We've been at Jedi Base 18 for two days now while all the Jedi masters have converged. Masters Mun, Sammeh, and Cor are here, and Master Ojiee is bringing the rest of the apprentices to help with the rescue. This is a major operation! Roikoan must be incredibly dangerous.

It was so good to see my friends again, even though telling me that I look tired wasn't the nicest thing Q-13 has ever said (definitely not the meanest, either). The thing is, they're not wrong. I'm exhausted. It feels like every time I close my eyes I have nightmares where Victor is calling out to me.

I feel absolutely certain that the real Victor is using the Force to guide me to him. It doesn't really explain the Wookiee arms, tho. That was upsetting.

Thanks to Master Ojiee's successful reconnaissance mission and the intel we have from Krio Vin we know the basic layout of Roikoan's base on Batuu, and we have a good idea as to where he is keeping Iyawa and her apprentice. What we don't know is why he's taken them or what he plans to do with them.

Lord Roikoan wants to lure me to him and he's using Victor as bait.

Why does he want you?

Because he wants his lapdog back.

Revenge. For the past year, Krio Vin has been supplying us with intelligence on Roikoan's operations. It was because of his information that we were able to take down Goonga the Hutt and I'gork Faul.

That was you?

I was working to make things right. I have a lot to answer for.

You certainly do.

If I see you so much as point this toward anyone on our side, I will end you.

So . . . is Mr. Zefyr just really mad that you went to the dark side? Because he seems angrier with you than everyone else here.

Including me.

Our feud predates my association with Lord Roikoan.

What did you do?

Nothing! He's the one that shot first.

Who did Mr. Zefyr shoot?!

No one, we were playing grav-ball, it was my turn to shoot the ball, but he went first, claiming it was his turn when it so clearly wasn't, and then things got out of hand and we lost the championship.

Wait, how long ago was this?

IT'S AS IF IT HAPPENED YESTERDAY!

Okay. This is RIDICULOUS. Both of you get over yourselves right now, we need to save Victor . . .

Christina, what do you feel?

We need to get to a lower level. Victor is deep beneath the surface where there isn't any natural light.

Good work.

And he's scared. He's acting like he isn't, but he is.

Well, that's most of us all the time.

It is.

twist

Let's go.

Victor?

Unhand my son, you fiend!

Oh, Krio. We used to be so close and now I'm a fiend? You've become so judgmental.

If you so much as hurt one hair on his head—

Me? Hurt Kaa Vhin? Perish the thought. He's free to do whatever he wants, aren't you Kaa?

I am.

And he wants to stay with me and be my apprentice, don't you, Kaa Vhin?

I do.

Victor, NO!

It's all right, sister. My name is Kaa Vhin now. Master Iyawa wasn't even supposed to be my master—she was my fifth choice, and if I stay with her I will never learn to climb to greater heights. Lord Roikoan can unlock my hidden potential, which is currently asleep at my center.

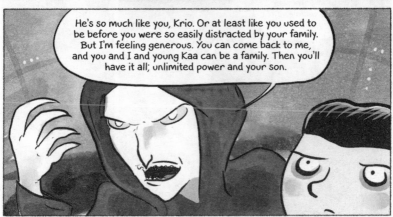

He's so much like you, Krio. Or at least like you used to be before you were so easily distracted by your family. But I'm feeling generous. You can come back to me, and you and I and young Kaa can be a family. Then you'll have it all; unlimited power and your son.

I...I...

Victor...

Hey, Roikoan? Can I call you Roi? Quick question.

Oh. Look. It's the girl Starspeeder.

Yeah, that's me. So why did you choose to take Victor and not me?

I mean, I think I'd make a pretty great Sith. Last semester I raised a wild nexu to be my pet. For fun.

Christina, what are you doing?

Go to the surface. No arguments!

Christina?

We can trust him, GO!

GIVE ME A BREAK. YOU WILLINGLY GAVE AWAY YOUR ENTIRE LIFE.
NOOOOOOOOO!!!
BOOF!

THE DAILY MILLENNIUM

MISSING JEDI MASTER AND APPRENTICE FOUND!

After weeks of being held captive by the nefarious Sith, Lord Roikoan, Master Iyawa and her young apprentice, Victor Starspeeder, have been rescued on Batuu.

"Victor was instrumental in his own rescue," said Jedi Master Skia Ro. "He was able to gain the trust of Roikoan by making him think that he had succumbed to the dark side, and then gave us a coded message letting us know where Iyawa was being held without anyone noticing."

"The whole operation was a real team effort," she went on, "which we couldn't have done without the help of Krio Vin, who gave us valuable intel on Roikoan's compound."

Krio Vin, the former Sith who escaped from his prison cell around the same time as Master Iyawa's capture, will be returning to Oovo 4 to complete his prison sentence.

MASTER YODA DEFEATS GOONGA THE HUTT IN VERY SHORT BATTLE ON CORUSCANT

With the Jedi Academy on Coruscant mostly emptied of staff and students, escaped convict Goonga the Hutt made a misguided attempt to take over the famous campus. Unfortunately, for him and his henchmen, Jedi Master Yoda had remained to guard the school.

"Wanted to build a casino here, he did," Yoda told reporters while waiting for authorities from Canto Bight to take Hutt and his cohorts away. "Foolish, he was, and also very weak. Eat more stickli root, he should. Good for stamina." Then the Jedi Master proceeded to give reporters his own recipe for mashed stickli root, which requires an alarming amount of bantha butter.

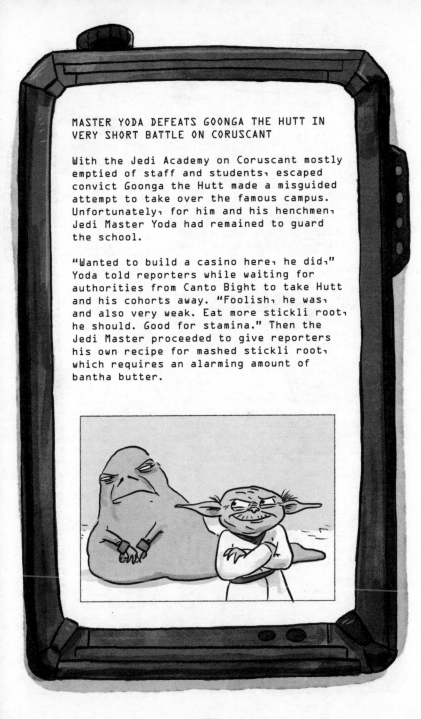

I have wanted to do this for SO LONG. This is the best day ever!

SNIP SNIP

Done!

Well?

No more cones?

Shaddap, Kaa.

You look just like your mother did when she was your age.

I don't think Mom ever won a battle with a Sith.

But she did. She fought me, and she saved you two from what I had become by running away with you. And then even though she knew you would be tempted by the dark side, she still let you go to Jedi Academy. She's the strongest person in the galaxy.

She made a great home for us.

I know. Listen, Roikoan was right when he said that I chose to give away my entire life. I did, and I know I can never get it back. If you never want anything to do with me ever again, I get it. It's what I deserve.

If you send me holomessages, I'll open them.

Me, too.

Hugs?

No.

But maybe one day.

MONODAY

We're finally back on Coruscant! And we're not the only ones. Once Yoda proved that he could single-handedly defeat Goonga the Hutt, I'Gork Faul, and a bunch of goons, all the Jedi Academy students returned to campus. Word must have gotten around that my friends and I were instrumental in the rescue of Victor and Iyawa, and now all the students are looking at us like we're already Jedi Knights or something. It's nice, I suppose, although it feels more like a huge responsibility. These kids are actually looking up to us, and I wonder if this is how our Masters feel all the time.

We're leaving soon, but Masters Iyawa and Skia Ro are taking Krio Vin back to Oovo 4 and letting Victor and me come along. But there's one last score to settle first.

So what now?

Back to Jedha to get your things.

Wait, why?

Because you're done. You rescued Victor by using the Force to find him. You stayed your hand and didn't strike Roikoan down in fury after you thought he'd murdered your father. You made peace with Krio Vin. I don't think there's much more I can teach you. You are a Jedi Knight, Christina, and you're ready to move on.

175

Jarrett J. Krosoczka is a *New York Times* bestselling author, a two-time winner of the Children's Choice Book Award for the Third to Fourth Grade Book of the Year, an *Eisner* award nominee, and is the author and/or illustrator of more than forty books for young readers. His work includes several picture books, the Lunch Lady graphic novels, and Platypus Police Squad middle-grade novel series. Jarrett has given two TED Talks, both of which have been curated to the main page of TED.com and have collectively accrued more than two million views online. He is also the host of The Book Report with JJK on SiriusXM's Kids Place Live, a weekly segment celebrating books, authors, and reading. His graphic memoir, *Hey, Kiddo*, was a National Book Award Finalist.

Jarrett lives in western Massachusetts with his wife and children, and their pugs, Ralph and Frank.

Amy Ignatow is the author and illustrator of The Popularity Papers series and the Odds series. She lives in Philadelphia with her family and really, really wants a lightsaber.

To all our Jedi Academy readers both young and old:
May the Force be with You, Always.